Amelia's Road

written by Linda Jacobs Altman
illustrated by Enrique O. Sanchez

SCHOLASTIC INC.
New York Toronto London Auckland Sydney

Text copyright © 1993 by Linda Jacobs Altman.
Illustrations copyright © 1993 by Enrique O. Sanchez.
All rights reserved. Published by Scholastic Inc., 555 Broadway,
New York, NY 10012, by arrangement with Lee & Low Books, Inc.
Book design by Tania Garcia.
Book production by Our House.
Printed in the U.S.A.
ISBN 0-590-14828-1

4 5 6 7 8 9 10   *09*   04 03 02 01 00 99

The illustrations are rendered in acrylic on canvas.
The text is set in 14 point Meridien.

To my husband Richard Altman,
por los caminos venideros — *L.J.A.*

To Kim — *E.O.S.*

Amelia Luisa Martinez hated roads. Straight roads. Curved roads.
Dirt roads. Paved roads. Roads leading to all manner of strange
places, and roads leading to nowhere at all. Amelia hated roads so
much that she cried every time her father took out the map.

The roads Amelia knew went to farms where workers labored in sunstruck fields and lived in grim, gray shanties. *Los caminos*, the roads, were long and cheerless. They never went where you wanted them to go.

Amelia wanted to go someplace where people didn't have to
work so hard, or move around so much, or live in labor camps.

Her house would be white and tidy, with blue shutters at the windows and a fine old shade tree growing in the yard. She would live there forever and never worry about *los caminos* again.

It was almost dark when their rusty old car pulled to a stop in front of cabin number twelve at the labor camp.

"Is this the same cabin we had last year?" Amelia asked, but nobody remembered. It didn't seem to matter to the rest of the family.

It mattered a lot to Amelia. From one year to the next, there was nothing to show Amelia had lived here, gone to school in this town, and worked in these fields. Amelia wanted to settle down, to belong.

"Maybe someday," said her mother, but that wonderful someday never seemed to come.

"Mama," Amelia asked, "where was I born?"

Mrs. Martinez paused for a moment and smiled. "Where? Let me see. Must have been in Yuba City. Because I remember we were picking peaches at the time."

"That's right. Peaches," said Mr. Martinez, "which means you were born in June."

Amelia sighed. Other fathers remembered days and dates. Hers remembered crops. Mr. Martinez marked all the important occasions of life by the never-ending rhythms of harvest.

The next day, everybody got up at dawn. From five to almost eight in the morning, Amelia and her family picked apples. Even though she still felt sleepy, Amelia had to be extra careful so she wouldn't bruise the fruit.

By the time she had finished her morning's work, Amelia's hands stung and her shoulders ached. She grabbed an apple and hurried off to school.

Last year, Amelia spent six weeks at Fillmore Elementary School, and not even the teacher had bothered to learn her name.

This year, the teacher bothered. She welcomed all the new children to her classroom and gave them name tags to wear. She wore a name tag herself. It said MRS. RAMOS.

Later, Mrs. Ramos asked the class to draw their dearest wishes. "Share with us something that's really special to you."

Amelia knew exactly what that would be. She drew a pretty white house with a great big tree in the front yard. When Amelia finished, Mrs. Ramos showed her picture to the whole class. Then she pasted a bright red star on the top.

By the end of the day, everybody in class had learned Amelia's name. Finally, here was a place where she wanted to stay.

Amelia couldn't wait to tell her mother about this wonderful day. Feeling as bright as the sky, she decided to look for a shortcut back to camp. That's when she found it.

The accidental road.

Amelia called it the accidental road because it was narrow and rocky, more like a footpath that happened by accident than a road somebody built on purpose.

She followed it over a grassy meadow, through a clump of bushes, and down a gentle hill. There, where the accidental road ended, stood a most wondrous tree. It was old beyond knowing, and quite the sturdiest, most permanent thing Amelia had ever seen. When she closed her eyes, she could even picture it in front of her tidy white house.

Amelia danced for joy, her black hair flying as she twirled around and around the silent meadow.

Almost every day, when work and school were over, Amelia
would sit beneath the tree and pretend she had come home.

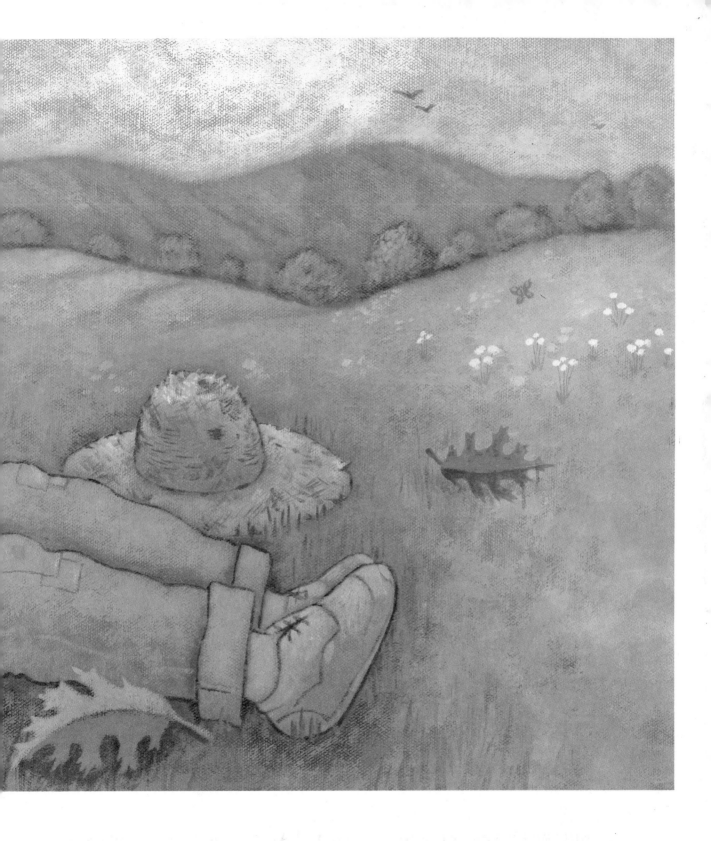

More than anywhere in the world, she wanted to belong to this place and know that it belonged to her.

But the harvest was almost over, and Amelia didn't know what she'd do when the time came for leaving.

She asked everyone for advice—her sister Rosa, her parents,

her brother Hector, her neighbors at camp, and Mrs. Ramos at
school, but nobody could tell her what to do.

The answer, when it came, was nearly as accidental as the road.

Amelia found an old metal box that somebody had tossed into the trash. It was dented and rusty, but Amelia didn't care. That box was the answer to her problem.

She set to work at once, filling it with "Amelia-things." First she put in the hair ribbon her mother had made for her one Christmas; next came the name tag Mrs. Ramos had given her; then a photograph of her whole family taken at her last birthday; and after that the picture she'd drawn in class with the bright red star on it.

Finally, she took out a sheet of paper and drew a map of the accidental road, from the highway to the very old tree. In her best lettering, she wrote *Amelia Road* on the path. Then she folded the map and put it into her box.

When all the apples were finally picked, Amelia's family and the other workers had to get ready to move again. Amelia made one more trip down the accidental road, this time with her treasure box.

She dug a hole near the old tree, and gently placed the box inside and covered it over with dirt. Then she set a rock on top, so nobody would notice the freshly turned ground.

When Amelia finished, she took a step back and looked at the tree. Finally, here was a place where she belonged, a place where she could come back to.

"I'll be back," she whispered, and then she turned away.

Amelia skipped through the meadow, laughed at the sky, even turned cartwheels right in the middle of the accidental road.

When she got back to the camp, the rest of the family had already started packing the car. Amelia watched them for a moment, then took a deep breath and joined in to help.

For the first time in her life, she didn't cry when her father took
out the road map.

Author's Note

Amelia Luisa Martinez and her family, and thousands like them, are often referred to as migrant farm workers. This is because they usually have to move from one harvest to another, and they do not have stable homes. Many of the migrant workers come from different parts of the world, such as Mexico, South America, or the Caribbean. But many of them are American citizens, born in the United States.

Some of the male workers travel by themselves and return to their families after the harvest. Others travel with their families. Out of necessity, even their children work in the fields.

The constant work and moving about make it very difficult for the children to get to know a place or to make friends. In this story about Amelia, my hope is to show how one girl finds a favorite place.